THE VIEWING ROOM

AN EROTIC ADVENTURE

VICTORIA RUSH

VOLUME 41

JADE'S EROTIC ADVENTURES - BOOK 41

COPYRIGHT

The Viewing Room © 2021 Victoria Rush

Cover Design © 2021 PhotoMaras

For the uninhibited...

WANT TO AMP UP YOUR SEX LIFE?

Sign up for my newsletter to receive more free books and other steamy stuff. Discover a hundred different ways to wet your whistle!

Victoria Rush Erotica

1

I initially heard about the club from a friend. A place where anonymous strangers could go for safe, clean, legal sex. Where the rooms were separated by a piece of clear plexiglass and you could get your freak on watching people on the other side doing the same.

At first, I found the idea mildly irritating, like why would people go somewhere to have sex when you can't even *touch* your partner? But as I lay awake in my bed getting hornier and hornier with each passing night thinking about it, my compulsion to investigate it further became overpowering.

How was it any different from the online webcam chats I'd become addicted to? Those were hands-free *too*, and I had no trouble getting off watching a whole train of sexy girls jilling themselves while I watched. In fact, this took it one step further. At least at this club, I'd be watching live performances in the *flesh*, separated mere inches from a real person. As I rubbed out one powerful orgasm after another, I contorted my body into different positions picturing my imaginary partner watching me thrusting my fingers into my wet pussy while I gushed all over the glass.

After three or four restless nights, I'd had enough. I had to at least try this place out to satisfy my curiosity. I was getting tired of having sex with myself and there wasn't exactly a line of hot chicks waiting at my door to jump into my bed. So one lonely night, I threw on a shawl and a head-scarf in an attempt to disguise my identity and went down to the club to check it out.

When I pulled up in front of the shop behind a suburban industrial mall, I was mildly surprised. This wasn't some kind of seedy operation tucked away in a dark alley with a burly doorman guarding a graffiti-covered door. The sign above the plate glass entrance read *Sightlines – An Adult Adventure Club*. Far from trying to hide their real purpose, this place seemed eager to advertise to any passerby what *really* went on behind closed doors.

I parked my car in a spot furthest from view from the road, then opened the front door noticing a smartly dressed man standing behind the polished counter.

"Welcome to Sightlines," he said, peering up at me with a warm smile.

"Hello," I stammered, awkwardly meeting his gaze as I smiled back at him nervously. "Um, this is my first time. How exactly does this work?"

"No worries," he said, passing a laminated brochure toward me and flipping it open. "You can choose between pay-as-you-go or monthly, annual, or lifetime memberships. The longer the term, the lower the effective price-per-use, but if this is your first time, you might want to choose one of the shorter plans to make sure you're happy with the experience."

"Uh-huh," I nodded, peering at the professional photos of scantily clad men and women looking suggestively across at one another in the spartan but clean-looking studios.

"Doesn't *everybody* leave here happy? I mean, isn't that the whole *point* of this place?"

"Well, yes," he said, clasping his hands in front of him. "But it can be a little–*jarring*–at first. It's not everybody's cup of tea."

"These rooms," I said, flipping through the pictures where all of the clients looked like a supermodel who'd just finished a carton of ice cream. "Are they safe? Not just from the person on the other side, but also from outside intruders. I wouldn't want to be interrupted once things start to heat up."

"Absolutely," he said. "The rooms are divided by a solid sheet of two-inch-thick glass that's virtually bulletproof. And each viewing room door is deadbolted from the inside. At least until your appointed time has expired, when they automatically release."

"How long do I have before *that* happens?" I said, crunching my eyebrows at the thought of the doors releasing in the middle of a hot mutual masturbation scene.

"Most rooms are set for a fifty-minute time release. Although you can choose shorter or longer intervals with the pay-as-you-go plans."

"What about the *sanitary* aspect?" I said, picturing the glass partition and grimy floor streaked with cum stains and other bodily fluids.

"All of the surfaces are coated in washable vinyl and acrylic laminate. After each session ends, the rooms are locked and receive a two-hundred-degree sanitary cleaning."

"Like in a car wash?" I said, looking up at him with pinched brows.

"A bit like that," he said. "Except we add a few other chemical additives like bleach and chlorine to kill any remaining microorganisms. You could eat off the floor if you chose to once the cleaning procedure is finished."

"I don't know about eating," I said. "But I can think of a few *other* things I might want to do down there."

The attendant peered back at me and smiled.

"Once you're in there with your partner, what you choose to do with each other is completely your business."

"And this is completely touch-free?" I asked. "I mean, it's just for *watching*?"

"That depends on how closely you want to engage with your partner. Each glass partition has a foldable portal that is locked on both sides. If you both desire, there are ways for you to engage more directly..."

"How large is this portal?" I asked, picturing some greasy guy reaching through and pinning me against his sweaty body.

"Just large enough to push your erogenous parts through," he smiled.

"You mean like a glory hole?"

"In a manner of speaking," he said. "How you and your partner choose to use it is your business. Many of our clients prefer to stay at a distance and just watch."

As I flipped through the pictures of the hot models and listened to the attendant explaining how everything worked, I could feel my panties beginning to moisten.

"Is this a full unisex operation?" I said, still harboring a few lingering doubts. "I mean, it's not just a bunch of guys showing their meat and jerking off?"

"All of our members have to schedule their visits beforehand, and we try to ensure a fairly even split of men and women between the six viewing rooms."

"What about the *walk-ins*?" I said, picturing half their

clientele comprised of horny businessmen stopping by for a quick wank.

"They're limited to two per hour unless we have extra capacity. But we're normally fully booked at this time of the day."

"Do you have room for one more walk-in?" I said, feeling a trickle of lubrication running down the inside of my thigh at the thought of choosing between six sexy partners.

The man turned to the computer terminal resting at his side and punched a few keys.

"We do indeed," he said. "Would you like to schedule a fifty-minute session to start?"

"That should do the trick," I smiled. "Do I have to sign a waiver or something?"

"No," he said. "We do everything we can to preserve our clients' anonymity. Will you be paying with cash or credit card?"

"I suppose if I want to remain *anonymous*, I should pay cash," I smiled, opening my purse. "What is your fee?"

"One hundred dollars for fifty minutes or seventy-five for twenty minutes."

"I'm pretty sure I'm going to need more than twenty minutes," I smiled, sliding five twenties across the counter. Something told me once things started to heat up in there, neither one of us would be in a hurry to get out.

The man processed my payment then handed me a plastic passkey and a folded white bath towel.

"This gives you access to the women's washroom where you can change and shower. The locks are on a timer, starting at the top of the hour for exactly fifty minutes. You'll have to vacate your chosen viewing room when you hear the buzzer to allow time for cleaning before the next session."

"Or you'll lock me in there getting a scalding hot shower?" I said, lifting an eyebrow.

"There are motion sensors in each room plus an emergency exit switch. But if you go over the fifty-minute allotment, there will be an additional charge to your account."

"Okay," I said, shaking my head at their rigid protocols. "It looks like you've really got this place locked down. Do you have security if there's any trouble?"

"We have two other attendants on duty, but it's very rare for them to be deployed. They're here more in case you happen to slip or fall, or have some other kind of emergency."

"Like if my partner's double-dildo goes too far up my ass?" I smirked.

"Something like that," he said, pressing a button under the counter and pointing to a door leading to the interior marked with the female cross-and-circle symbol. Before passing through the door, I noticed a *third* door marked with the transgender symbol.

I smiled, feeling my pussy beginning to tingle as I walked down the long corridor toward the women's change room.

These guys seem to have covered all the bases, I thought to myself.

2

———

When I slipped my passkey into the door lock, I was pleasantly surprised when I entered the bright and spacious ladies' room. Clad in white tile and alabaster marble, it gleamed under the bright overhead lights. Four or five women milled about the room in various stages of undress. A pretty brunette was placing her street clothes in the bank of lockers next to me while the others stood in front of the large mirrors over the vanity primping and preparing their makeup.

I couldn't help staring at their sexy asses as they bent over and checked their makeup. A cute redhead peered back at me and I blushed, embarrassed to be seen using the facility. I glanced at my watch, realizing I only had twenty minutes to get myself put together and turned toward the lockers, opening the one on the far end.

As I began to disrobe, I glanced in my peripheral vision at the brunette placing her clothes in the locker next to me, wondering how much I should remove. I wasn't sure if people entered the rooms stark naked, or wore their undergarments or dressed up special for the occasion. When I noticed her putting on a high-cut bikini bottom and a tight-fitting tube top, I peered over at her with a puzzled look.

"Is this your first time, honey?" she said with a slight southern accent, noticing my hesitation.

"Yes," I said. "I wasn't exactly sure what people wear for this sort of thing."

"Well, eventually, *nothing*," she smiled back at me. "But you don't want to go in there buck naked. You never know what you're going to run into on the other side. It could be a sweaty old fat dude who's just looking for a cheap thrill. Besides, half the fun is playing the game. You want to hold a little bit back at the beginning so you can build the excitement and rise to an exciting climax."

"I didn't bring anything special," I said, drinking in her voluptuous figure as I ran my eyes over her skimpy two-piece outfit showing off all her curves. She was about average height with a slender build, but she had oversize tits pressing against the stretchy fabric of her bikini top. I could clearly see the bumps protruding from the fabric as her erect nipples winked at me from the other side of the bench.

"I wouldn't worry about it, sweetie," she said, appraising my own figure clad in lacy panties and bra. "That should do the trick just fine. Nobody's going to be judging you for the clothes you're wearing. But that ensemble ought to attract their attention right quick."

I jumped when I heard a loud buzzer echoing through the change room.

"What's that sound?" I said.

"It's signaling the end of the hourly session when everybody has to clear out of the viewing rooms to allow enough time for cleaning. You definitely don't want to have your shower in there."

A few moments later, three naked women came through

the change room door, carrying their loose change of clothes in their hands. I noticed each of them looked flushed with a slight sheen of perspiration covering their bodies. One was an athletic-looking blond, one was a curvy African-American woman in her forties, and the last one was a young Hispanic girl looking barely out of her teens.

But they all were sexy and hot. The brunette next to me noticed me staring at the ladies as they retrieved their towels from their lockers and headed to the bank of showers on the other side of the room.

"You like the little ones, do you?" she said, noticing me following the Hispanic girl's ass into her stall.

"I don't have any preference really," I said, feeling my face beginning to flush again in embarrassment.

"But you like *girls*?" she said.

"Sometimes," I nodded.

"When you get out there, look me up. I'll be in room six at the end. I'd be happy to put on a show for you."

"Okay, I said, closing my locker door as the second alarm signaled the official start of our scheduled session. I followed the brunette to another pair of doors marked *Viewing Rooms*. She placed her passkey in the door for Bank A and pulled it open.

"Which one do I use?" I said.

"Whichever one accepts your card," she said. "I've already pre-scheduled a room, so I'll be in the hall on the A side."

I pressed my card into the slot under Bank B and a green light went on as I heard the door lock unlatch.

"See you on the other side, sweetie," the brunette said. "Have fun!"

I could feel my heart pounding in my chest as I began to walk down a long corridor while two women followed behind me and three men entered from the other side. On the left-hand side was a row of open doors, each leading to a bright white-washed room with another person sitting on the other side of the glass.

As I walked past each door, I peered into the room, noticing a different person in various stages of undress. In some of them it was a man wearing little or no clothing, whereas others held a woman peering back. Some of the men were already hard, showing off their turgid erections as they stroked themselves slowly, whereas the women were more covered up, reposing in various stages of seduction.

Behind the second door I saw the attractive redhead from the change room, lifting up one side of her tight t-shirt, revealing the plump curvature of her left breast. I almost face-planted into the open door jamb of the next viewing room holding a hunky guy flexing his abs while he rolled his hips, flapping his large, half-erect cock from side to side. The third room had another woman I recognized from the change room, a pretty blonde about my age peering back at me seductively as she licked her upper lip slowly, trying to entice me into the room.

My pussy was saying yes, but my mind wanted to wait until I had evaluated all the options before deciding. The next room housed a slightly older man with a smooth but taut body and a bit of gray hair up around his temples. He was attractive in a rich executive kind of way, and I could feel my panties dampening as I hesitated once again outside his door. But I'd remembered the pretty southern belle from the change room saying she was in the last cubicle, and my racing pulse egged me on.

When I peered into the last room and saw her squeezing her tits while she sat on a clear acrylic chair spreading her legs apart, I looked behind me noticing all the other clients had already ducked into one of the other rooms, closing the door behind them.

I guess it'll be the pretty brunette then, I nodded to myself, entering the chamber and latching the door behind me.

The room was larger than I expected, and spotlessly clean. Every surface was either covered in floor-to-ceiling mirrors, white laminate, or gleaming floor tiles. The surfaces were still steaming from its recent antiseptic wash, with light drops of dew running down over the walls and toward the center of the room where a chrome drain plate lay on the floor. Placed exactly halfway in the middle of the room was a huge glass partition extending from one side wall to the other and from the floor to the ceiling, with a tight cement bond securing it at each edge. The glass was perforated with two rows of small horizontal holes around eye and knee level, which I assume was designed to facilitate conversation between the two sides.

There were also two larger circular holes cut out of the glass about four inches in diameter spaced about a foot apart, looking like the ideal place to thrust one's breasts if the mood struck. About a foot and a half below that, there was a rectangular slice about six inches tall and three inches wide. The perfect spot to insert a hard dick, I thought, smiling to myself. Or a wet pussy. The setup reminded me a bit of those wooden cut-outs you sometimes saw at county fairs where people stuck their arms and faces through the holes to make themselves look like cowboys or farm animals.

"I hoped you'd make your way down here," the brunette said, pulling off her stretchy top to reveal her magnificent tits. They were huge and pointy, seemingly suspended in midair by marionette strings. "My panties have been wet from the moment I first saw you."

"Mine too," I said, taking a seat in the acrylic chair facing toward her, only four feet apart between the glass wall.

"I like fresh meat," she purred, running her eyes up and down my quivering body. "You look good enough to gulp down in one serving. Show me those nice titties under that girly bra."

"What about taking our time and building the excitement?" I smiled. "I thought you said there was some kind of *art* to this thing?"

"We've only got fifty minutes," she said. "I'd rather use the time soaking up your beautiful body and pleasuring myself. Don't be shy, it's just you and me."

I peered up around the edge of the ceiling to make sure there were no hidden cameras, then slowly pulled off my bra and hung it over the back of my chair.

"Yes, baby," the brunette purred. "That's what I'm talking about. That's a pretty nice set of ta-tas you're sporting. Pinch your nipples and bounce them up and down for me so I can see how firm they are."

I rolled my fingers over each of my nubs feeling them hardening then I cupped my hands under each breast and shook them gently.

"Damn, girl," the brunette sighed. "Those are *real*, alright. Nice and firm and outstanding. Very lickable. Do you like having your tits sucked on by another girl?"

"Sometimes," I lied, feeling my nipples pressing out further from my swelling areolas.

"I can tell this isn't your first rodeo," she said. "Is your *lower* half getting just as worked up watching me sitting here half naked?"

"Um-hmm," I nodded. "But it would get a lot *more* excited if you'd take off your clothes and show me your magnificent figure in all its glory."

"*Now* who's in a hurry to get all down and dirty?"

"Like you said," I grinned. "We've only got fifty minutes. More like *forty* now..."

The brunette stood up off her chair and lifted her hands over her shoulders, pulling her stretchy top off her body and throwing it on the floor. I gasped when I saw her pointy tubers sticking straight out from her taut stomach like a pair of fat bombs. As she swung her shoulders from side to side, her enormous melons swayed and slapped together.

Those aren't fake tits, either, I smiled, rocking my hips in synchronicity with her on my moistening chair. *No plastic surgeon in his right mind would make tits that unique and out of proportion.* But her voluptuous shape was just getting me more turned on as I began to feel a small puddle forming in the center of the acrylic chair between my legs.

"You *like*?" she said.

"Uh-huh," I nodded in a trance.

"Come to the glass," she said, bending her finger toward me as she placed her naked body up against the partition, poking her pendulous tits through the two circular holes.

"Mmm," I purred, walking up to the glass and inhaling her puffy areolas into my mouth, one at a time.

"Fuck yes," she moaned. "Suck on your momma's titties. Suck my teats like you haven't eaten in days."

You have no idea, I thought to myself, suddenly remembering how long it had been since I'd tasted the sweet flesh of another woman.

As she writhed against the sturdy glass, I encircled her spongy tits through the holes and squeezed them hard while suckling on her nibs like a ravenous newborn.

"Fuck, baby," the brunette panted. "You really know how to suck a girl's tits. I could do this all day if you let me."

"Oh?" I said, coming up for air long enough to peer at

her with a raised eyebrow. "There aren't any *other* parts of your body that need attention?"

"If you're offering, I'll accept," she grunted, pulling her tits out of the holes with a plop and bending down to open her side of the vertical portal. I did the same, and when she had a clear path of entry, she mashed her dripping cunt against the opening while I fell down on my knees, lapping her folds up and down like an ice cream cone.

"Oh *Gawwd*," the brunette groaned, buckling at the knees and threading her fingers through the upper holes to support her sagging weight. "Suck my pussy baby. Lick your momma's cunt. I've got a *different* kind of nourishment I want to give you now."

I tilted my head up trying to stimulate her flaring clit, but the angle of her straightened body against the perpendicular glass and the configuration of the narrow opening made it difficult for me gain traction. Getting more and more worked up by my flicking tongue, the brunette threaded her fingers through the small holes at shoulder level and lifted her feet off the floor, spreading her legs up and to the side of the glass.

As her pussy tilted upwards toward my face, I slid two fingers into her slit and began caressing her G-Spot. She groaned louder, pressing her hips harder against the glass as she lifted her straightened legs even higher. By the time I engulfed her burning bulb in my mouth and began sucking on it hard, her body was jackknifed against the glass, quivering against my face as I lopped up her juices and twirled my tongue around her jewel like a spinning top.

I have a feeling this isn't *her* first rodeo either, I smiled, feeling her pussy beginning to tent as she edged closer toward climax.

"Oh my God, baby," she growled. "Suck my cunt with

everything you've got. I'm going to come all over your sweet face. Keep massaging my G-Spot. I'm getting close."

"Mmmm," moaned, burying my face between her dripping folds. I was eager to use the newfound techniques I'd recently learned at the Fountain of Venus masturbation workshop to see if I could make her ejaculate all over my face.

"*Oh fuck, oh fuck...*" she grunted. "It feels like I'm going to pee. But I can't stop it. I'm sorry hunny, I'm going to pee all over your face!"

I nodded excitedly encouraging her to release it, knowing it wasn't actually urine she'd be releasing but the built-up prostate fluid from her Skene's Gland that I'd been stimulating with my fingers inside her pussy.

"Let it go, baby," I murmured while gnawing on her twitching clit. "Come all over we. Let me feel you shower me with your love."

Although *love* was probably the furthest thing on her mind right about now, I wanted to do everything I could to encourage her to release whatever inhibitions might be holding her back. I peered up and noticed her red fingers gripping the airholes in the glass in a vice-grip, when suddenly she pressed her cunt hard against the glass and began hollering at the top of her lungs.

"Uhnnnn," she groaned as her pussy clamped down hard on my fingers and clear jets of fluid began squirting out both sides of her flapping lips. "I'm cumming, baby! Oh God–I'm cumming like I've never come before. Drink my juices, baby!"

Knowing she was ejaculating clear prostate fluid instead of urine, I was only too happy to swallow her sweet cum while she pounded her hips against my mouth in the narrow opening and squirted her juices all over my chin and down my chest and abdomen. As I held her twitching clit in my mouth while pressing my two fingers hard up against her swollen G-Spot, I closed my eyes tasting and feeling the pleasure pouring out of her.

Then the loud buzzer sounded, jolting us out of our carnal bliss.

3

———

That night I could hardly sleep reliving the experience of sucking the pretty brunette pinned up against the shaking glass. I hadn't even removed my panties the whole time, I was so absorbed in giving pleasure to my viewing room partner. But I was determined to go back as soon as possible and this time make it a true two-way experience. Maybe I could find the same girl and have her reciprocate the pleasure I'd given her. God knew I was ready to spray all over her pretty melons.

I returned to the club the next day around the same time, hoping the brunette was thinking the same thing. When I pulled open the front door, the attendant peered up at me and smiled.

"Hello again," he said.

"Hello," I smiled back.

"I assume you enjoyed your first experience at Sightlines?"

"I did indeed. But we kind of got cut off earlier than I expected. Is there some way I can buy a *longer* session this time?"

"Absolutely. If you're willing to pay, you can have the room as long as you like."

"I think two hours should just about do it. Do I get a discount for booking a longer session?"

"Unfortunately not," he said. "We're almost booked up solid, so the regular hourly rate applies."

Two hundred bucks was nothing to sneeze at, but it seemed a veritable bargain compared to what I'd have to pay to have live sex anywhere else, especially this clean and safe.

"Have you got room for another walk-in?" I asked.

He turned to his terminal and tapped a few keys, peering at the screen.

"In one hour, yes."

"I'll take it," I said, counting out the cash I'd already put aside for the visit.

After processing my payment, he handed me another passkey and a folded towel.

"You can go into the change room early, but your card will expire at the end of the next hour. Remember to exit the viewing room when you hear the buzzer."

"It's pretty hard to miss," I smiled. "Especially when your mind and other body parts are distracted doing other things."

The attendant nodded, and I turned to enter the door leading to the ladies' change room. Since I had a little more time before the session got started, I decided to have a shower to get myself in the mood. There were a couple of other women milling about the room, but no sign of the sexy brunette. As I stepped into the shower stall and felt the pulsating jets bouncing off my skin, I felt a charge running through me, wondering who I'd be paired up with this time.

There was something about the waist-high glory hole that particularly excited me, and as I slipped my fingers into my dripping pussy, I wondered what it would be like to feel a throbbing *cock* pounding me from the other side. Whoever it was this time, I was determined to get as good as I gave. Two hours was plenty of time to experiment with all manner of maneuvers, and the more I thought about the different ways my partner and I could engage with each other, the more excited I became.

I came two times fingering myself under the warm spray, and by the time I emerged from my stall, the room was filled with three more women preparing for their turn in the viewing rooms. I didn't recognize anyone from the previous day, but there was plenty of interesting candidates to pair up with. I noticed some of the girls talking amongst themselves at the makeup mirror, already forming alliances. I removed all my clothes and placed them in the locker, then I walked up to the mirror buck naked and leaned over to touch up my mascara. A few of the girls glanced at my upturned ass, peering at the dark shadow between my legs while I peered back at them beguilingly.

Two can play this game, I thought. I didn't want to be left on the short end of the stick with a stubby old fat guy as my partner if I could help it. If I could select my partner beforehand and identify her cubicle number, all the better.

But before long, the buzzer marking the end of the last session sounded, and a new stream of women began filing into the change room from the other side. As before, they looked slightly disheveled and flushed, with happy grins on their faces as they shuffled into the shower to clean up after their viewing room experiences. I noticed the cute Hispanic girl from the previous night and she glanced my way, staring at my ass before ducking into one of the stalls.

Okay, I nodded. *There's some regularity to the clients' schedule after all.* I made a note to return tomorrow an hour earlier to see if I could catch her before she escaped again into someone else's clutches. Not long after, the second buzzer sounded, and the first batch of girls exited through the two doors to the opposing viewing halls. As before, there was a bit of a dash down the hall while all the men and women peered into the six rooms to see who they wanted to pair up with.

But unlike yesterday, when I took my time sauntering to the last room, this time it was a much faster process choosing my partner. When I reached the third room, I stopped in my tracks staring at a gorgeous blonde peering back at me from the other side of the glass partition. With plump pouty lips, blue eyes, and wavy platinum hair, she looked like a dead-ringer for Marilyn Monroe. But it wasn't just her *face* that made my pussy throb in anticipation, it was her amazing figure.

Just like the movie star, she seemed to have perfect hour-glass proportions, with firm, bouncing tits, a narrow waist, and long, sensuous legs. But it was what I saw at her *midsection* that stopped me cold. Dangling between her partially parted legs and hanging a good eight inches over the edge of the chair was a beautiful, long, semi-erect penis pulsing excitedly as she teetered on the edge of her seat. I ducked into the room before the line of approaching men from the other side of the hall could get a glance at her and quickly latched the door behind me.

"Hi," the pretty girl said.

I didn't know if she had transitioned from boy to girl or girl to boy, but at this point it hardly mattered. Other than the huge python hanging between her legs, she otherwise looked one hundred percent woman to me.

"Hi," I squeaked back, suddenly feeling my entire body tingling with goosebumps.

"You're very pretty," she said, running her eyes up and down my naked body while I stood dumbstruck in front of the glass like a kid in a candy store.

"So are you," I lamely echoed.

"Do you like girls with dicks?" she said.

"I do *now*," I smiled. "I've never seen anyone so beautiful and so well...*endowed*."

"Is this your first time with a ladyboy?" she purred, spreading her knees further apart as her gigantic organ began to rise in jerky pulses.

"No," I said, reflecting back on my last encounter with the pretty cabaret dancer, Shae. "But it's been far too long."

"Mmm," she said, staring at my protruding nipples and shaved mound. "You must attract them like flies with that body. But I suppose you prefer the real *he-man* types, captain of the football team and all that."

"I can go both ways," I said, sitting down in my chair to quiet my quivering legs. "I actually prefer girls, but I enjoy a real dick inside me once in a while."

"Instead of a fake dildo?"

"Yeah."

"You like my big fleshy cock?"

"Yes," I panted, feeling another pool of lubrication beginning to form in the center of my chair. "Wrap your hands around it and let me watch you rub it for a few moments."

"Mmm," she moaned, wrapping two fists around her joystick as she began to pump it hand-over hand.

"Jesus," I muttered under my breath, shocked at the size of her now fully-grown erection. I'd watched enough men jerking off in my day, but somehow watching this beauty gripping her pulsating pole while staring back at me with her pretty lips parted took me to a whole new plane.

I thrust three fingers into my sopping slit and began

ramming them in and out of my cunt while I watched her milking her meat like a giant cow's udder. I noticed a bead of precum forming on the top of her purple crown and begin dripping down over the sides of her hands, and I groaned feeling my own juices running down the insides of my thighs.

"Do you like watching ladyboys beat their meat?" she asked.

"Ye–yes," I panted, feeling the pleasure beginning to spread throughout my body.

"Do you like watching us spray our loads all over our titties?"

"Yes," I said. "But I like it even better when you pump it inside my pussy. I wouldn't want you to waste any of that sweet nectar by spilling it on the floor."

"Don't you worry about my getting it back *up*, if you're worried about that," she said. "I could probably come *five times* before I lost interest in fucking you."

"Well then, I'd kind of like to watch you spray your come all over your pretty tits, after all. Your cock is more impressive than any man's I've ever seen."

"Oh yeah?" she grunted, squeezing her buttocks and tilting her cock even higher above her body. "What exactly do you like to do with a real cock?"

"Pretty much everything," I panted, locking my eyes on her enormous pecker. "Hand jobs, blow jobs, taking from the front or the back, between my tits, you name it. It's a beautiful thing to play with. I've often fantasized about having one myself."

"Oh, the things I could do with you if you had a lady-cock," she groaned, shaking her head. "I'd love to slap my dick against yours and rub our cocks together while we watch each other spurting all over our tits."

"Yes, baby," I purred. "Show me what that's like. I want to watch you spurt all over your pretty tits. Show me how a real ladyboy gets off."

"Fuck girl," she grunted. "You're a little bit dirty, aren't you? I like it that way. My balls are getting itchy. Are you getting close too?"

"Yes," I said, feeling my body beginning to tense up before I passed the point of no return. "Come for me. Let me see how high you can shoot in the air."

"Fuck, yes," she grunted, angling her hips forward and clenching her buttocks until she was almost levitating off the chair. "Here it comes, baby. I'm going to cum so hard..."

I could see her gripping her dick so hard that it was creating white marks around her knuckles, then she threw her head back and howled as her balls tightened around the base of her hands and her legs began flapping in and out.

'Uhnnnn," she growled with a new deepness to her voice as long ropes of thick white cum began shooting up into the air far above her body.

I could actually hear the first jet splatter off the ceiling as it showered back over her while she spurted one long string after another in decreasing arcs over her quivering tits and stomach. As I watched her erupting like a volcano on the other side of the glass, I pulled my fingers out of my cunt so she could see me spraying my own juices almost as far out toward her, coating the glass on my side with long rivulets of clear fluid.

"Holy fuck!" she exclaimed when she saw me spraying my ejaculation in tandem with hers while we both jerked and spasmed in our shaking chairs.

It seemed to take almost a full minute for the two of us to stop quivering and convulsing in our dripping chairs, and when we finally spent all of our juices, we slumped in our seats staring at one another.

"Jesus, girl," she said. "I take that back about wanting you to have a dick like me. You don't even *need* a cock to ejaculate. Where did you learn that trick?"

"I've been doing it for quite a while actually," I smiled. "Perhaps I missed my calling. Maybe this means I'm coming back as a man in my next life."

"If you do, you'll inseminate more women than Genghis Khan with your prodigious output. I've never seen a woman gush like that before in my life."

"Same here," I winked back at her.

"I don't know about you," she said, standing up to show me her still-hard cock while peering at my glistening pussy. "But I'm ready to put this thing somewhere a little warmer and wetter. And I can see a perfect spot standing only a few feet away from me."

"That's not the *only* thing that's warm and wet," I said, rubbing my dripping hands all over my breasts. "Come up to the glass where I can see that thing a little better."

We approached the partition from opposite directions and when we reached the wall, she pressed the underside of her pole against the transparent glass as we pressed our mouths through one of the titty holes, flicking our tongues in each other's mouths.

"God, how I wish I could rub my body against yours right now," she said, peering at my tits mashed up on the other side of the glass.

"I'm sure that can be arranged later," I said. "But let's make the best use of the time we have while we've got it. Push your dick through the gloryhole and let me touch it. I want to feel that firehose coursing through my hands."

"I thought you'd never ask," she said, flipping her side of the portal covering open while I did the same.

When she pressed her organ through the hole, I gasped appreciating the enormity of it for the first time. Easily as thick as a soda can and twice as long, it looked more like a horse's cock than a human's. I inspected it closely, running my fingers along its length like a tailor measuring the inseam of a man's pants. More than twice the length of my outstretched fingers, I estimated it to be almost twelve inches long and eight inches around.

"Holy fuck," I said. "That is one impressive instrument you've got here. How do you manage to get that inside anyone? It looks like it would be better suited inside a *horse!*"

"You're not the first one to make that comparison," she said. "But as long as you're sufficiently lubricated, it can pretty much fit anywhere."

"I'm looking forward to that," I smiled, peering up at her. "But first, do you mind if I give you a little handy of my own? I've never felt a man's or a woman's cock this big before, and I just want to admire it for a few moments."

"Knock yourself out. Just watch out when it's time to spurt. I wouldn't want to knock you over or anything."

"Mmm," I said, wrapping my fingers around her enormous shaft. "I'd love to feel you spray all over my face and my tits. I haven't enjoyed a cock like this in a very long time."

"You mean one this *big?*" she said, threading her fingers through the airholes at the side of the glass as I began to massage her giant phallus.

"I mean any one at all. I almost forgot how much fun it was to play with these things. I've pretty much only been with women these past few years."

"Well, you're with a woman *now,*" she said, rocking her big dong in and out of my clasped hands.

"Yes, a very well-*endowed* woman. What a beautiful sight it is to see a girl displaying her excitement in such an obvious way. And you're not just *big*, your cock is actually quite beautiful."

"You better stop or you're going to make my head swell."

"It's *already* swelling," I said, peering at her purple crown pouring precum all over my hands while I caressed her perfectly straight spear.

Suddenly, I stretched my lips over her swelling tip and sucked her into my mouth, flicking my tongue around her sensitive rim as I bobbed my head up and down.

"Oh, *God* yes," she groaned, peering down at me while I sucked on her like a lollypop. "That feels way better than my hands."

"Mmm," I hummed, hoping to add a little extra degree of stimulation to her throbbing prick.

As she began to hump her hips against the glass being careful not to impale me with her long sword, I traced one hand a little lower and cupped her balls, circling my little finger in the sensitive area under her perineum.

"Fuck, girl," she panted. "You're full of surprises, aren't you? For someone who professes to prefer girls, you sure know how to give an expert blowjob."

"Mmmft," I grunted, barely able to breathe with her giant organ stretching my mouth, let alone talk.

I could feel the escalating pace of her humping action and her balls growing tighter the closer she got to orgasm, and for a brief moment, I considered allowing her to come in my mouth. But it wasn't the fear of her dumping her enormous load down my throat that gave me pause so much as desperately needing to feel her inside me, pounding my aching cunt. I didn't want to take any chance that she'd lose some of her hardness or enthusiasm for the final act.

I popped my mouth off her pole and I watched it bouncing excitedly a few inches from my face as it poured a river of precum all the way down her long shaft and compressed balls.

"You're absolutely *wicked*," the girl groaned, dry-humping the space in front of my licking lips. "You're just going to make it worse when I finally bend you over and give you a proper fucking."

"Promise?" I said, standing up and turning around to position my ass toward her flapping pole. "Because if I don't feel you inside me pretty soon, I'm going to explode. Besides, this *other* part of me is better suited to stroking that monster anyway."

"We'll have to see about that," she said as I tilted my hips upward and positioned her slippery head against my dripping lips.

For the first time, I was happy to have an artificial barrier between the two of us, so I could direct how much of her cock was inserted into my pussy lest she try to ram the whole thing inside me, which I was sure would split me in two as sure as an axe through brittle wood. I had to use all the strength in my leg muscles to push back hard enough for the tip of her tool to spread me apart and begin sliding inside, and when it finally did, it felt like I was delivering a baby. Stretched to my maximum limit, I eased myself backwards until I filled my tunnel with as much of her beanstalk as I dared. When she had about two-thirds of it embedded inside me, we slowly began rocking our bodies together while I placed my fingertips on the floor to keep me from falling over.

"God damn, that's a beautiful sight," she said as she plowed her cock inside me. "I haven't seen an ass that pretty in long time.

"It must look like a cherry impaled on a pool cue," I panted, feeling the tip of my clit dragging across the base of her shaft from my stretched labia. "I can barely believe you got it inside me."

"Oh, it's *inside* you alright," she panted. "And it's a beautiful sight. It's too bad you can't see it for yourself."

I peered between my legs trying to see her shaft piledriving into my ass, but other than her tight balls slapping against my swollen lips, I couldn't see much. Realizing that I risked giving her a heart attack from all the false starts, I leaned forward and slowly pulled her out of me, making a loud popping sound as her pecker sprung free over my dripping ass.

"*What the fuck*?" she groaned. "You better make up your mind pretty quickly how you want to finish this, or I'm going to have to take matters into my own hands and spray all over the glass once again. You're driving me crazy!"

"I'm sorry babe, but you got me thinking. We *both* should be watching this to fully appreciate the experience. I want to see that big pole going in and out of me while I'm riding you. Can we do it facing one another this time?"

"Okay, but only if you promise this will be your last switch-up. You're not the only one who's about to explode here."

"I promise," I said, grabbing hold of her upturned dick flapping through the portal and pressing it down a few inches as I raised myself up on my tiptoes and slowly lowered myself onto her joystick.

"Uhnnn," we groaned together as my sheath enveloped her giant organ. I wasn't sure how much I could get inside me from this angle, and fearful of her pounding up against my cervix, I placed my two biggest toes of each foot in the lower row of holes and spread my knees apart while I gripped the upper holes with my fingers for support.

As I began bouncing up and down on her like an ape, we both began grunting as we peered at one another through the glass. She pressed her body closer to the surface and we joined our mouths in one of the tit-holes, kissing passionately while we fucked each other through the smaller portal below.

There was something incredibly sexy about being joined at the hips but separated otherwise by the hard barrier of the glass partition. As we writhed our sweaty bodies against the slippery surface and peered at one another through the transparent panel, I could see the rising ecstasy rolling over her face as she began to pound her hips more forcefully against the wall. The strange combination of erotic sensations was having the same effect on me, and as I looked down to watch her giant phallus pistoning in and out of my stretched pussy, I relaxed my grip and lowered myself fully onto her burning staff.

As I began to feel my pussy expanding around her big prick, my pleasure crested like a roller coaster, and I felt my built-up tension pour out of me as I gushed all over her balls while she howled through the glass, emptying her seed inside me. It must have been a hell of a sight with the two of us pinned to the glass and me holding on to it like a climber hanging on for dear life, while my partner clung to her side of the glass just as tightly as we both quivered and convulsed with a steady stream of juices pouring down over the partition on both sides and circling quietly into the drain in the middle of the floor beneath us.

4

———————

The buzzer signaling the end of our session sounded not long after the T-girl and I climaxed together, then we returned to the change room to exchange phone numbers and head our separate ways. I was annoyed with myself for not getting the brunette's phone number from the previous night, but I hoped I'd see her again soon. Although I suspected many of clients preferred the anonymity of the experience and left the facility soon after they finished their business, for me it was turning out to be a great place to meet new playdates.

After returning home later that night, my whole body was still buzzing from the exciting hookup with the ladyboy. Even though my pussy was a bit sore, I was already looking forward to my next visit to the club, wondering who'd I'd meet next. There was something incredibly exciting about not knowing who I'd encounter in the secretive viewing rooms, and the unexpected liaison with the sexy ladyboy had taken the experience to a whole new level.

I returned to the club the following night around the

same time, hoping to find some of the women I'd been keeping my eye on during the previous visits, but I was also eager to try out a new stranger.

"Hey," I nodded to the attendant after opening the front door and strolling up to the front desk.

By now, most of my nervousness about using the establishment had evaporated, with the two of us treating it like any other type of business transaction.

"Hello," he said, smiling up at me. "Glad to see that you're enjoying the experience enough to become a regular. Do you want to look into signing up for one of the longer-term plans?"

I paused for a moment, not sure I was ready to make this a recurring habit. The novelty still hadn't worn off, and I didn't want to use the club as a crutch for building a more meaningful, long-term relationship.

"Not quite yet. But the two-hour walk-on suits me just fine if you space again tonight."

He checked his computer again and nodded.

"You're just in time to catch the last nine p.m. slot," he said, sliding a passkey across the desk and handing me another clean bath towel. "I guess you know the drill by now."

"Yup," I said, opening the door toward the ladies' change room. "Keep an eye on the clock to make sure I don't get caught with my pants down, and clear out of there when I hear the buzzer to avoid getting an unwanted car wash."

I smiled heading down the hallway, thinking these guys had created quite the gravy train. If they were legit about being booked solid most of the time, one hundred bucks an hour for two people in six separate viewing rooms added up to almost thirty grand a day for an operation that ran twenty-four-seven. *Pretty good gig, if you can get it.*

When I opened the door to the change room, I recognized a couple of women from the previous two nights, including the sexy redhead and the athletic-looking blonde. But the T-girl and the brunette were nowhere to be found, and I stepped into the shower to clean up in preparation for the next session. When I came out a few minutes later, I noticed the cute Hispanic girl from two nights ago staring at me in the reflection of the make-up mirror.

I patted myself dry then walked over to the mirror pretending to wring out my hair, but really I just wanted to get a closer look at her body. While I ran my fingers through my hair and pushed it away from my face, I glanced down at her tight figure, admiring her small but firm breasts, well-toned stomach, and tight ass. Her pussy was shaved as bare as a baby's bottom, and as she leaned over the mirror to apply some bright red lipstick on her lips, I noticed the nub of her clit peeking out at the base of her mound.

She caught me staring, and I blushed when our eyes made contact in the mirror. I was tempted to ask her which room she'd be using tonight since I'd noticed her coming from the reserved rooms on the A side of the hall previously. But mindful of everyone's privacy, I fidgeted in front of the mirror for another five minutes, feeling my juices running down the inside of my thighs as I fantasized about watching her touching herself on the other side of the glass. When the buzzer sounded signaling the start of our session, she placed her hand on mine and peered into my eyes.

"I'm in room six," she said in a sexy voice. "Look me up. I've got something special I've been saving for you."

I gaped at her with an open mouth, not quite sure what to say, then she disappeared down the hallway marked A, and I quickly followed down the opposite hall, not wanting anyone else to get to her first. I didn't even look into any of the other viewing rooms as I made my way down the hall, I was so focused on getting to her room before anyone else. I crossed my fingers as three men emerged from the men's change room side, but thankfully after glancing into room six, they continued down the hall. When I reached her room, I was surprised to see it empty, but not wanting to miss my chance at scooping her up, I stepped inside and quickly latched the door closed behind me.

I took a seat in the still warm, steaming chair and crossed my legs, enjoying the pleasant sensation of the freshly cleaned acrylic surface pressing against my tingling folds. After half a minute or so, the door on the other side opened and the cute Latina girl stepped inside, totally naked. My pussy fluttered when I saw that we'd be alone together in our own room, but I flinched when suddenly another man walked in behind her. He looked to be of similar age and ethnicity, slim but ripped, with a partially erect cock that swung seductively from side to side as he ambled into the room behind her.

The girl smiled at me as she led him to the chair and sat him down, then she kneeled in front of him with her back toward me. Dispensing with any preliminaries, she proceeded to take his dick into her mouth and begin fellating him while she angled her ass toward me, spreading her legs about a foot apart. Her backside was blocking my view of her partner's cock, but judging from how high her head was bobbing above his rocking hips, he must have been pretty well endowed.

The young man moaned as he ran his fingers through her hair, peering up at me with a look of bliss on his face. When she threaded a hand between her legs and began massaging her vulva while sucking her boyfriend, my own legs began to part involuntarily as my fingers drifted over the crest of my pelvis toward my dripping cunt. I could hear both the young man and the girl moaning on the other side of the partition, and it didn't take long for me to join them with the sound of my own grunts and sighs.

I was enjoying the sight of two lovers having sex more than I expected, and before long I had three fingers planted inside my pussy as I spread my legs wide apart on the edge of my chair. Whether I was excited because I could only see his handsome face as his girlfriend worked him over or because I was eager to see his fully erect tool or because she had the most magnificent tight ass I'd see in ages, I wasn't sure. All I knew was that I was enjoying the show tremendously, and within seconds I could feel the familiar sensation of another rapidly approaching climax welling up inside me.

The girl must have heard my increasingly loud and urgent moans from the other side of the glass, because just as I was about to come, she suddenly stood up and turned around to face me, sitting down on her boyfriend's cock. I had just enough time to see that it was a good eight inches long with a lovely caramel color before it slipped inside her shaved twat. She slid down slowly over it, taking it one inch at a time, until her glistening slit rested directly overtop his tight balls.

Then she placed her hands on top of his thighs and began to pump her body up and down on his flexing pole. As excited as I was watching her servicing him with her back turned, this new display was a million times hotter. As I watched her tits flushing and the insides of her thighs growing increasingly slicker from the juices pouring out of her pussy, I rammed my fingers harder into my snatch, circling my clit with my other hand. The man reached around from behind her and squeezed her breasts, sucking on the side of her neck while he peered sexily into my eyes.

During the entire display, my gaze darted between their enraptured faces and his glistening pole and her swollen slit. It was a feast for the eyes, and I stared unashamedly at the two of them while jerking in my chair, feeling my orgasm approaching like a freight train. When it finally hit me, I groaned loudly, flapping my legs in and out as I jetted long streams of clear cum toward the glass. When they saw me squirting in the throes of climax, the man grunted and pulled the girl harder toward him, burying his cock deep inside her quivering pussy. With the three of us now deeply immersed in a powerful orgasm, we locked eyes on each other, wailing in unison as we jerked our bodies in simultaneous pleasure.

When the couple finally became still, the young girl smiled toward me, scooping up the slick lubrication coating the inside of her thighs and spread it all over her pretty tits and erect nipples. I did the same, pinching and twisting my nipples to make them harder, and after another minute or so, she raised herself off her boyfriend's cock, letting it flap against his stomach. The tip of his cock rested almost an inch above his belly-button, with a gentle convex curve that made his dripping helmet press against his belly.

"Would you like a piece of my boyfriend's cock?" the girl said, noticing me staring at his hard-on.

"Yes please," I said, feeling my pussy fluttering at the thought of being filled a little deeper.

"Come up to the glass," she said. "I want to watch him fucking you."

I walked up to the partition and flipped open my side of the lower portal.

"Do you want it from the front or the back?"

"From the back first," she said with a glint in her eyes.

The young man eagerly thrust his dick through the hole and I turned around and bent over, angling my pussy up toward his glistening crown. When I felt the tip beginning to spread my lips apart, he suddenly lurched forward, and I grunted feeling him fill my void. As he began to rock his hips against my ass pressed up against the glass, I felt his girlfriend's hand slide underneath his balls and squeeze the base of his shaft while he plowed my depths.

"Do you like that baby?" she teased. "Do you like fucking this hot momma's pussy while I watch?"

Even though I was probably only ten years older than them at best, I smiled at her suggestion that I was old enough to be their mother. But far from turning me off, it actually got me even more turned on.

"Uhhnn," was all he could manage to groan as she squeezed his balls and teased the underside of our perineums with her fingers.

"Do you want to feel her squirt over your balls while I hold your dick in my hand?"

"Yes," he panted more deeply, approaching another climax.

Although the girl's dirty talk was getting me just as worked up, it was the action of her hand caressing our joined body parts that put me over the edge. I'd never felt this strange combination of sensations before, and the fact that we were separated by the hard barrier and I was turned in the other direction made it all the more titillating. When I felt her slip two fingers inside my pussy beside her boyfriend's thrusting dick, I squeezed down hard, pushing my pent-up juices all over her boyfriend's balls, her hand, and my quivering legs. As I began to jerk my body in the throes of another powerful orgasm, her boyfriend groaned in ecstasy, pressing his cock as deep into me as he could. Even though I couldn't see anything turned away from the couple, somehow it was even more erotic listening to their reaction coming from the other side of the glass.

"Yes, baby," the girl purred. "Come inside her sweet pussy. Feel her juices coating your balls. Are you enjoying your birthday present so far?"

"Fuck yes," he grunted, feeling my warm pussy enveloping his twitching prick.

"*Birthday*, hmm?" I said, pulling myself off him after we'd both stopped shaking. "Is this your first time in a three-way?"

"Um-hmm," he nodded, his cute face still flushed in a post-orgasm glow.

"Well, we're going to have to give you the full treatment then," I said, not bothering to point out that I'd already noticed his girlfriend visiting the club two times before. Whether she was coming alone or with someone else or with his blessing to test the waters, I wasn't sure. But knowing it was his first time with two women suddenly made our little affair all the more interesting. "How exactly would you like it? Would you like to watch me eating out your pretty girlfriend, or watch us grinding our pussies together, or would you prefer me to suck you off while your girlfriend watches?"

"Um..." the boy hesitated, overwhelmed by the choice of equally compelling options. "All of the above?"

His girlfriend and I chuckled at his innocent enthusiasm, then I peered at them for a moment, trying to figure out how we could make this work.

"I have an idea, if you guys are game," I smiled, making a mental note of the position of the lower hole and the two breast holes. "You look like you're in pretty good shape. Why don't your girlfriend and I rub our pussies together while we face each other against the glass, and you stand on your hands with your cock poking out one of these upper holes while I suck you off? That way, you can have a bird's-eye view of what's happening down below while your girlfriend watches me giving you head right next to our faces?"

"Okay," he said, not thinking about it for very long. I'm sure neither of them had dreamed of trying anything so kinky, and neither had I for that fact.

"Are you up for it too, sweetheart?" I said, glancing toward his girlfriend.

"Are you *kidding* me?" she said with her eyes agape. "That sounds insanely hot!"

"Okay," I said, pressing my body up against the glass with my dripping pussy positioned over the lower portal. "We're going to have to do this carefully. We don't want anybody to get hurt here."

"You can handle it, *right* baby?" the girl said to her boyfriend. "You work out at the gym. This should be a piece of cake for you."

"Yeah," he said. "But I've never done handstand pushups while someone was sucking my dick."

"We're not exactly expecting you to do multiple sets or anything," she said. "All you have to do is hold yourself up while we do all the work. And something tells me you won't have to hold the position for very long. I have a feeling this is going to pop your nut pretty quick."

The girl placed her body against the glass facing me, then she pushed her hips forward, grinding her mound against mine through the lower portal. When we were in position, her boyfriend squatted behind her and placed his feet against the partition between her hips, then slowly inched his feet up the wall until they were pointing straight up over her head. We had to scrunch down a few inches to make room for his flapping cock above her shoulder, then we tilted a few inches to the side to give him enough room to poke it through the right titty-hole.

When he thrust it through the opening, I immediately took his member into my mouth while his girl watched with her face pressed against the glass only a few inches away. As we slowly began to grind our mounds together a few feet below, the three of us began to groan from the sensation of being joined together in carnal bliss against the transparent barrier.

At first, I was so excited by the sheer audacity of what we were doing that I felt an electric charge running through my body as the three of us began to twist and rub our bodies against one another. But it didn't take long for the girl and me to realize that the vertical position of our bodies pressed up against the glass with our mounds touching through the narrow opening was making it impossible to angle our pussies in such a way to gain any friction on our clits. While the two of us helplessly rolled our hips against the glass, the boy happily groaned away bobbing his cock through the upper opening into my eager mouth.

Birthday or no, I thought, *we girls deserve to be enjoying this as much as he is.* She must have been thinking the same thing I was, because after a minute or so of awkwardly grunting and twisting our bodies together, she paused and looked down toward her boyfriend.

"Are you enjoying the *view* down there, baby?" she said.

"Definitely," he panted. "This is way better than I pictured it in my mind."

"I'm glad *one* of us is getting his jollies from this little gymnastics maneuver. But we girls are having a bit of a tough time stimulating our pussies from this angle. Do you think you've got enough strength to raise one hand and place it through the hole under our crotches to stimulate our clits?"

"I'll try," he said, grunting as he tilted his body, placing all of his weight on one arm while he pushed his other hand through the glory hole.

I felt his palm sliding over our labia, and when his fingers reached the bump of my swollen clit, he pinched it between his fingers and began to rock his hand back and forth between our legs.

"Yes, baby," his girlfriend moaned. "Just like that. Press the palm of your hand against my pussy while you stimulate her clit with your fingers. Are you able to support yourself doing this?"

"For now," he huffed, obviously straining near his physical limit. "But I don't know how much longer I can stay in this position."

"That's okay," she said, peering at me rolling my eyes in pleasure from the sensation of rubbing our mounds together while he trilled our clits with his free hand. "I have a feeling you won't need to for very long."

As she scrunched her cheek against the glass watching me suck her boyfriend's reddening dick pumping through the upper hole, we mashed our tits together against the partition, grunting more loudly. Her boyfriend's expert jilling of our pussies a few feet below was having the desired effect, and as the three of us began groaning in tandem, I couldn't help smiling out the side of my mouth at the craziness of what we were doing. But it didn't take long for my mirth to transform into ecstasy as I began to feel the rising tide of pleasure building within my body. This was the sexiest sixty-nine position I'd ever been in, and the simple novelty of it was quickly bringing me to the edge of my cliff.

"Let it go, baby," the girl panted, seeing the look of ecstasy wash over my eyes as her boyfriend humped my mouth more vigorously. "Dump your load in her mouth. I'm going to come with you. Get ready to watch us gush all over your face and hand when we come. Are you ready?"

"Fuck yes," he grunted from below. "Oh fuck–*here it comes!*"

As I began to feel him spurting his warm seed into my mouth, I peered into his girlfriend's eyes while she watched his dick pulsing around my lips, and her mouth gaped open hitting the crest of her own pleasure.

"Oh fuck, baby!" she groaned. "I can see your cock pulsing. I'm coming with you! Can you feel my contractions?"

Suddenly, I felt the muscles of my pussy clamping together and I began gushing even harder than I had the previous two nights, as a torrent of juices squirted out of me all over the boy's hand and face buried in his girlfriend's ass. As the three of us grunted in unison in a powerful simultaneous orgasm, we struggled to hold our positions trying to maintain contact for as long as possible.

When we all finally stopped shaking, the boy pulled his dick out of the upper hole and fell backwards onto the floor as his girlfriend and I collapsed beside the glass in a puddle of fluid. When we finally stopped panting and recovered from our intense climaxes, we peered over at one another and started laughing. We'd just performed an equal part comedy, action, and skin flick all rolled into one crazy, audacious escapade. I didn't know if anyone was keeping track of the all the unusual ways the club's clients interacted in these strange viewing rooms, but surely the three of us had set some kind of high mark for an acrobatic performance.

---

*R*eady for more erotic chills and thrills? Preorder the exciting first story in Victoria Rush's new erotic fantasy series, *The Enchanted Forest:*

Sometimes it's not just the grass that's greener on the other side...

FOLLOW VICTORIA RUSH:

Want to keep informed of my latest erotic book releases? Sign up for my newsletter and receive a FREE bonus book:

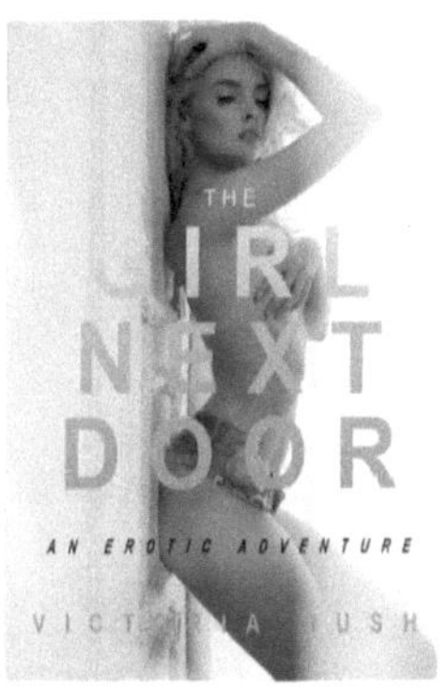

Spying on the neighbors just got a lot more interesting...